NIÑO'S MASK

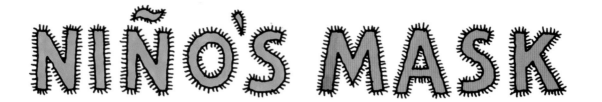

Jeanette Winter

DIAL BOOKS FOR YOUNG READERS NEW YORK

To Roger,
who knocked at the door

Published by Dial Books for Young Readers
A division of Penguin Putnam Inc.
345 Hudson Street, New York, New York 10014

Copyright © 2003 by Jeanette Winter
All rights reserved
Designed by Jeanette Winter and Atha Tehon
Hand-lettered by Jeanette Winter
Additional text set in Frutiger
Manufactured in China on acid-free paper

1 3 5 7 9 10 8 6 4 2

Library of Congress Cataloging-in-Publication Data
Winter, Jeanette. Niño's mask /Jeanette Winter.
Summary: Told that he is too young to wear a mask at the Fiesta, Niño
makes his own mask and surprises his family and the whole village.
Includes a glossary of Spanish words.
[1. Masks—Fiction. 2. Costume—Fiction. 3. Festivals—Fiction.] I. Title.
PZ7.W7547 Ni 2003   [E]—dc21   2001049912

The art for this book was created using felt-tip pens.